They say the apple doesn't fall far from the family tree.

It's sad, but true.

Don't get me wrong; not every hand-me-down trait is a bad one. After all, I've been told that I get my musical talent from my mom. And if you'd heard us at last year's mother-daughter talent show, you'd believe it. We dressed up in these fashion-forward hot-pink cleaning outfits and belted out the lyrics my mom had written for us:

Mom: *She never listens.*
Me: *She's right, I never listen.*
Mom: *And never does chores.*
Me: *I never do chores.*

Uh, okay, so the lyrics are kind of . . . lame. But you'll just have to trust me: We sounded awesome.

As for my dad, I'll give you three guesses as to what I get from him. Maybe this little memory will give you a clue. Picture it: Dad and I are sitting at the kitchen table as Mom places a plate of delicious, fresh-baked cookies in front of us. Sounds perfect, right? Just wait.

"Sue, you know I don't like nuts in my cookies," Dad complains, making a face just before he takes his first bite.

"Honey, those are raisins," Mom corrects him. "I haven't put nuts in the cookies since the night of our high school prom. Remember? The big vomit stain on my dress?"

No, that is *not* what I get from my dad. Keep waiting.

"Oh." Dad takes a bite out of the cookie and smiles. Then he spots something on the floor. "There's a raisin there, by your foot."

Mom bends down to pick it up, and . . . it scurries away!

There's a pause. Dad and I look at each other, the same thought racing through both of our minds.

"BUUUUUUUUUUUG!" Dad screams, jumping out of his chair. "Get it! Get it!"

Just Deal

Adapted by Robin Wasserman

Based on "The Rhinoceros in the Middle of the Room"
written by Sue Rose and
Based on "The Balancing Act" written by Laura McCreary

Based on the television series *Unfabulous* created by Sue Rose

SCHOLASTIC INC.

New York   Toronto   London   Auckland   Sydney
Mexico City   New Delhi   Hong Kong   Buenos Aires

I hop up and leap into his arms, clutching him and shrieking, "Someone get it, *please!*"

Yes, I admit it — I'm afraid of bugs. The thought of some creepy-crawly creature climbing up the leg of my pants or across my forehead can keep me awake at night. I even hate picnics — too many ants. And let's not even talk about the day I was assigned to feed crickets to our class iguana.

And for this, I guess I have only my dad to thank.

But the biggest, most obvious, most awful family gift of all doesn't come from either one of my parents. It comes from Aunt Bertha. Aunt Bertha, with her frumpy flowered dresses; her mop of stiff, curly gray hair that feels like a Brillo Pad . . . and her two big buckteeth. They make her look like a bunny rabbit, and they make her talk like this: "Oh, Addie, when you have af many molars af we do, floff is your friend." When I was a kid, Aunt Bertha liked to floss her teeth in front of me, to show me how it was done. "Fee that?" she would say, waving the cruddy string in my face. "That's roast beef."

Don't get me wrong: I love Aunt Bertha. I love everything about her — except those teeth. Because those teeth are *my* teeth. And if it weren't for my new mouthful of braces, I'd probably be introducing myself as "Addie *Finger.*"

That's right — thanks to the miracle of modern dentistry, I can get rid of Aunt Bertha's teeth.

Unfortunately, not everything can be fixed as easily as teeth.

It had been one heck of a week. And just when I thought it was finally over, when I thought I could finally just relax and enjoy myself, *it* happened. And it happened in front of the whole school. And it's not like nobody noticed — you'd think they would be watching the basket-ball game, but no. They were watching me. I mean, I was slumped in the bleachers with my head in my hands, but I could still hear them. I could hear what they were saying!

"It's too sad," Cranberry St. Clare said. She smoothed down her hair and checked to make sure that her designer sneakers didn't have any flecks of dirt on them. "I mean, we can't even make fun of her." "Her" meaning *me*.

"How long do you have to wait before you can say those pants make her butt look big?" her best friend, Maris Bingham, asked.

I heard that, too, and you know what? I didn't even have the heart to check and see if she was right. I was too freaked out.

I've gone through some rough times before. Who

can ever forget that one horrible day last year when everything just fell into place? The wrong place.

I raced into school about thirty seconds before the bell rang and practically slammed into my best friends, Geena and Zach, who were waiting for me by our lockers.

"Nancy barked all night," I panted, "the alarm didn't go off, Ben hogged the bathroom for at least an hour, and by the time I got downstairs for breakfast, all that was left were olives . . . *olives*! Could this day get any worse?"

That's when I took off my coat. And Geena's and Zach's jaws dropped.

"Um, yeah," Geena said quietly. Too quietly. "You're not wearing any pants."

Zach whipped out his jacket for cover, but it was too late — half the school had seen me in my Miss Piggy boxers.

"All right, all right," Zach had said gruffly. "Move along, rubberneckers!"

He's a good friend, but he couldn't stop them from laughing and pointing or calling me Miss Piggypants for the next two weeks.

But you know what? Even wearing boxers to school

hadn't prepared me for this one terrible week. And it definitely hadn't prepared me for that moment at the basketball game when I totally lost it.

"That girl is a loose cannon!" Duane Ogilvy whispered to his girlfriend, Mary Ferry. You guessed it: He was pointing at me.

"Well, at least she remembered to wear pants," Mary pointed out.

Enough! I jumped up from the bleachers. "I *overslept!*" I shouted. "Okay?"

They just shrugged and walked away. And I slumped back down in my seat. What was the point? I had bigger things to worry about. Things like Aunt Bertha. There I was, sitting in the bleachers, just peacefully watching a basketball game. A totally normal day, or so I thought. That's when I saw her, Aunt Bertha — down on the court, stuffed into a Rocky Road Middle School basketball uniform, calling for a pass. I mean, of course it wasn't really Aunt Bertha; it couldn't have been because —

Well, I guess before I get to that I should go back to the beginning — all the way back to that last Sunday dinner.

The third Sunday of every month is Singer Sunday Supper. Or, as Aunt Bertha would say, "Finger Funday Fupper!"

6

This particular Sunday was like all the rest of them that had come before. Aunt Bertha sat at the head of the table. Her buckteeth shined. And Mom, Dad, my brother, Ben, and I sported brand-new, hand-knitted sweaters, courtesy of Aunt Bertha. Mine was bright red with some kind of lumpy, misshapen animal galloping on a rainbow. It was going *way* into the back of my closet as soon as Aunt Bertha was gone.

Aunt Bertha's really my great-aunt — my dad's mother's cousin, or something like that. And she just *loves* Finger Funday Fupper.

"Fue, this ftew if fabulouf!" she cried, gulping down another mouthful.

Life's never boring when Aunt Bertha's around. She's not afraid to say anything. No subject is off-limits — and, believe me, no one's safe.

"Oh, and Fue," Aunt Bertha continued, grinning. She has this amazing smile; it's so big, you think it's going to break her face in half. "I faw the cutest little poodle dog, and it looked just like you!"

Everyone burst into laughter at the thought of a fluffy little dog walking around with Mom's face — everyone except Mom.

"Oh, it was a very, very beautiful poodle, though, right?" Dad said quickly, trying to stop chuckling.

But Aunt Bertha was already distracted by another thought. "Ben, ftill e-mailing pictures of your muscles to your girlfriend?"

That would be Tara, Ben's *ex*-girlfriend. She moved to California, wrote him a bunch of gushy love letters . . . and then she dumped him.

"Uh . . ." Ben's face turned red. Then he suddenly pointed to me. "Addie has a new boyfriend."

Traitor!

"Ben!" I cried. What ever happened to sibling loyalty?

"Oh?" Aunt Bertha leaned toward me, her face lighting up again with that grin. She loved a good story, especially a *love* story. "What happened to Jake?"

Now it was time for me to turn red. "Jake wasn't my boyfriend, Aunt Bertha. As usual, Ben doesn't know what he's talking about."

That's Jake, as in Jake Behari. And I have to admit that, until recently, I definitely wanted him to be my boyfriend. Desperately. I mean, he's cool, he's totally cute, and it turns out that he's actually a really nice guy. But I'm done with all of that now. Jake did tell Zach that he liked me, but he had just broken up with Patti Perez. She's one of the popular girls at school, but she's mean, too. I guess it turned out that dating her was a big mistake. Still, I don't think that meant Jake *really* wanted to date me. He was just on the rebound. Anyway, we're just friends now. And, uh, I kind of like someone else.

"Addie, tell me about this new boy," Aunt Bertha prodded. "Have you kiffed yet?"

Kiffed?

Oh . . . she meant *kissed*.

Oh, gross! Like I was going to discuss that at a family dinner!

And also . . . no. I hadn't.

But before I could say anything — and it's a good thing, since I was too stunned to speak — my dad jumped in. "Whoa, Aunt Bertha, no, there's no kiffing, uh, kissing, going on," he babbled. "Right, Addie? No kissing. None-what-so-ever."

"Uh . . ." What was I supposed to say? No, there was no kissing going on. Not yet, at least. But that didn't mean I wasn't holding out hope for the future.

"Addie likes Randy Klein," Ben butted in. Ben and his big mouth.

"Ben!" I shrieked. "I do not!"

Okay, I did, but I didn't know if he liked me.

"Kiffing can be very painful when you're wearing braces," Aunt Bertha cautioned. I wondered how she would even know, because it seemed pretty obvious she'd never worn any herself. "It can hurt like the dickens."

This was *not* where I wanted the Singer Sunday Supper conversation to go. My mission: to change the subject — immediately.

"Thank you so much for the sweater!" I gushed, clutching for something, anything, that would get us to stop talking about kiffing. I mean kissing. "The rhinoceros is *so* cute."

"A rhinoferous!" Aunt Bertha threw her head back and guffawed. "It's a unicorn," she corrected me. "Addie, you are too precious."

She threw her arms around me and pulled me into a big, warm hug. Now, let me explain something. Hugging Aunt Bertha is like . . . well, there's nothing like it. She mashes your face against her chest, so tightly that you're almost suffocating, and it feels like you're smothered in something warm and gooey. But at the same time, there's this safe, cozy feeling, like as long as her arms are around you, you're protected from anything the world can throw at you.

That is, until she spots a plate of cannoli and drops you like a hot potato.

"Oooh, cannoli," Aunt Bertha gushed, grabbing one off the plate and stuffing it into her mouth whole.

"They are my favorite. All this talk about kiffing has made me hungry."

After dinner that night, I was inspired.

I went upstairs, shut myself up in my room, pulled off the itchy wool sweater, and tossed it on the floor, then I got out my guitar. My mother may use her musical talent to sing about mopping floors, but for me, it's all about playing the guitar. I sing, too — about everything. Whenever anything important happens in my life, I make up a song about it. And, to tell you the truth, I make up songs about most of the unimportant stuff, too. It's just who I am.

I'd been writing lyrics in my head all through dinner, so once I got upstairs, I was ready to go.

Aunt Bertha, Aunt Bertha, there's no one better,
If you like buckteeth and rhinoceros sweaters.
I know she means well,
But as far as I can tell,
She knows nothing of kissing with braces.
(And if she did, I wouldn't want to know.)

But at the thought of kissing with braces — or worse, the thought of all the things that could go *wrong* when kissing with braces — I couldn't concentrate on my song anymore. I put down my guitar, visions of split lips and trips to the emergency room dancing through my head. What if I tried to kiss someone — someone like, say, Randy Klein — and his lip got stuck in my braces? I would never, ever live it down.

There was only one thing to do. Well, two things, if you thought finding a pair of pliers and ripping off my braces one by one counted as a real option. I guess I wasn't that desperate. Yet.

So anyway, back to Plan A. I flipped open my computer and did a search for "braces" and "kissing," hoping maybe to come up with some helpful tips. Here's what I came up with instead:

Headline: KISSING WITH BRACES NIGHTMARE!
Headline: WIRED FOR LIFE!
Headline: FROM HOT DATE TO DENTAL DISASTER!

Guess what? Not helpful.

My dog, Nancy, moaned in sympathy with me, which made me smile until I saw where she'd chosen to make her bed. Right on top of Aunt Bertha's red wool rhinoceros sweater.

"Oh, Nancy, you can't keep the sweater," I warned

her, wishing that she could. "Mom'll probably make me wear it to next month's Funday Fupper."

I sighed and picked up my guitar again. So much for the Internet — nothing to do now but sing the blues.

Aunt Bertha, Aunt Bertha, she was right,
Wires poke your gums, rubber bands do bite.
Thanks to orthodontics and heredity,
Who in the world will want to kiss me?

Nobody, that's who.
Or at least, so I thought.

The next morning we finally finished our unit in social studies. It had dragged on *forever*.

"Can you believe we spent a whole hour on the Louisiana Purchase and not one word about shopping?" Geena complained as she, Zach, and I filed out of the classroom.

"I didn't notice," I admitted. "I was thinking about . . ."

"Oh, let me guess," Geena said when my voice trailed off. "Randy Klein?"

"No. Maybe. Yes." Actually, I had been doodling all over the back page of my notebook. "Do you think Randy cried at *Finding Nemo*?" I asked Geena. That's what I was thinking about until I started drawing our names.

Geena stopped walking and grabbed me by the shoulders, forcing me to look her in the eye. "Look,

Addie, you clearly like him. When are you going to stop avoiding him?"

"I'm not avoiding him," I protested. "I'm just giving him some space."

That's when Geena reminded me of when we saw Randy in the hall last week. Before he could spot me, I made a quick getaway, hopping on the back of Principal Brandywine's motorized scooter and letting her carry me away.

"Ms. Singer, this is my *scooter*, not the number nine crosstown shuttle!" she shrieked as we rode off down the hall.

"Okay, so that *one* time," I admitted.

And that's when Zach reminded me of when we saw Randy in *Juice!* café two weeks ago. When I saw him, I was up at the counter picking up my smoothie and my muffin — two seconds later, I was gone. I disappeared in a flash of speed, just like the Roadrunner. Gone so fast, I left my smoothie and my muffin hanging in midair, like it took them a moment to realize I wasn't holding them anymore — then they dropped to the ground. Or so I hear — it's not like I was around to see it.

"Okay, so *two* times. But I'm not avoiding him. I swear."

And that's when Geena pointed down the hall

behind me. Randy was rounding the corner at the end of the hall and coming toward us. Smiling that adorably goofy grin. And looking right . . . at . . . me.

The lights snapped off and, suddenly, a loud roar and a powerful wind filled the hall. The helicopter descended and aimed a spotlight right at me. The rope ladder dropped down, and I grabbed it, holding on tight as my rescue chopper carried me away.

Or at least that's what I wish would have happened. So okay, I admit it. I'm totally avoiding him. What can I say?

"I don't want to look like I'm stalking him," I said defensively.

"There's a big difference between 'stalking' and 'stalling,'" Geena pointed out.

"Yeah, what are you waiting for?" Zach asked.

"I don't know — I just get nervous when I'm around him. What if he doesn't *like* me, like me?"

"What if?" Zach narrowed his eyes and lowered his voice — that's what he always does when he's about to give us a motivational lecture, which he does often. "What if I never went out for basketball? What if Geena never . . . what if she never . . ." He turned to Geena in confusion. "What do you do?"

Geena just rolled her eyes and ignored him. Too bad — because that meant she was still focused on me and my little . . . problem — on the fact that I was totally chicken. "The point is that you're never going to find out how Randy feels about you if you're afraid to be in the same room as him."

"Maybe. I'll think about it," I promised her. Maybe. Someday. A *long* time from now.

"Well, don't think too long," Geena cautioned, "'cause here he comes."

Uh-oh.

"Hey, Randy!" Zach greeted him with a high five.

"Hey, Zach. Congrats on last week's game, man."

"Yeah, thanks. It's a team effort." His modest smile turned into a wide grin. "All the team has to do is get the ball to me."

"Randy, why don't you come to this week's game with Addie and me?" Geena said quickly. "That'd be fun, right, Addie?" There was a pause. "Addie?"

But of course, there was no answer. Because I wasn't there anymore.

"I can't hear you!" I cried over my shoulder as I pushed through the doors at the end of the hall. "I'm running away!"

Later on, Geena told me about the look on Randy's face when he saw me disappear once again. She said he looked like one of those puppies in the cage at the front of the pet store. You know, he had the look the puppy gives you when it realizes that instead of taking it home, you're putting it back in the cage and going to *Juice!* to get a smoothie.

Geena just smiled back weakly. "She . . . likes to run."

I thought about what Geena and Zach said, and it made sense, but when I got home, any thought I had about Randy Klein just flew out the window.

When I walked into the kitchen, my mom and dad were both home, which was weird enough. And Ben was sitting at the table, his eyes red, plowing through a box of tissues. That was more than weird. That was freaky. I guess I should have known right then, but I didn't. I wasn't at all prepared for what came next.

Maybe that's why, when my mother actually said it, I just stared at her. I didn't get it.

"Oh, honey, I know this is a shock," Mom said. That's when I noticed that her eyes were red, too. And I realized something for the first time: There's nothing scarier than seeing your parents cry. They're supposed to be able to handle anything, right? They're the ones in control; they're the ones supposed to be taking care of *me* when *I* cry. I couldn't stand to look at her. But where else was I supposed to look? At my big brother, who was wiping his eyes and sniffling into his snotty tissue? At my dad, who just kept shifting his weight from one foot to the other and shaking his head, like he didn't want to be there but couldn't figure out anywhere else to be? So I just looked at the floor.

"What do you mean 'gone'?" I asked. Even though I knew the answer. I *knew*. "Gone where?"

That's when Dad spoke, for the first time. "Aunt Bertha passed away, honey."

I didn't know what I was supposed to do. Was I supposed to cry? I didn't *feel* like crying. I didn't really feel anything. I just —

Passed away? It didn't seem real. How could it be real?

"That's impossible," I protested, as if maybe there'd just been some big mistake and now that I was home, I could explain it all away. "She was just here."

Dad put his arms around me and held me tight, and I could feel him trembling a little. I pulled away. I didn't want to see Dad weak like that. I didn't want to see tears dripping out of Mom's eyes. I definitely didn't want to hear Ben wailing.

"Sweetheart, everyone grieves in their own way," Dad told me. He didn't try to hug me again.

"Your father and I are here if you want to talk," Mom said.

"Give it some time to sink in," Dad added.

"Let us know if you have any questions," Mom finished.

Any questions? I had about a million. Like, what was I supposed to do now? How was I supposed to feel? How come everyone else was crying, and I was just . . . me? Same old Addie, ready to go on with the day as if nothing had happened. Was there something wrong with me? And how long was everyone going to be all weird like this? How long would it be before things could go back to normal? Was it bad that I was still worrying about the math test I had to study for and wondering what to wear to school tomorrow? Was I supposed to be thinking about . . . other stuff?

But I couldn't ask any of that.

"I do have one question," I said slowly. "Can I get out of school if a great-aunt dies? Just —"

"Great-aunt?" Ben boomed, his voice hoarse from

crying. "She was the *greatest* aunt." He blew his nose loudly.

"On second thought, I think I'll stay in school," I said. And I went upstairs. I had to get away from my family. And stay away from them until they all stopped acting like crying zombies.

"It'll sink in," I heard Dad say as I was going up the stairs. I shut the door. Nancy was curled up in the corner of my room, her head buried in the itchy wool sweater. Aunt Bertha's sweater.

"Hey, Nancy," I told her, "it's your lucky day. You can keep the rhinoceros sweater!"

That's the last sweater Aunt Bertha will ever make for me, I thought, waiting for the words to mean something. Maybe this is when I would start to cry. Maybe then I could go down and join my family. After all, I loved Aunt Bertha just as much as the rest of them. But . . . no tears. And I still didn't feel anything. Except maybe a little relief that I would never have to wear the rhinoceros sweater again.

The next afternoon, Geena, Zach, and I went to *Juice!*

Maybe you're wondering why I was out with my friends, rather than hanging at home, aka depression central. Well, my mom said I could do whatever I felt like I needed to do. And I felt like I needed to go hang out with my friends at *Juice!*

Besides, it was depressing enough, don't worry.

"Bambi's mother," Geena said as we sat down with our smoothies.

"Charlotte," Zach added.

"Hansel and Gretel."

"They didn't die!" Zach protested.

"They did in the Grimm version," Geena argued. "They got baked in the oven."

"That was the witch."

"Oh." Geena frowned for a second, but then her face lit up with revelation. "Buffy."

"That doesn't count," Zach complained. "Willow resurrected her. She came back all wrong. It was depressing."

I couldn't take it anymore. *"This* is depressing," I cut in. "Why are we even talking about it?"

Zach and Geena exchanged a glance — one of those heavy looks that makes you know they've been talking about you, like you're some issue they have to deal with. I didn't like it.

"We're discussing our experiences with death — to help you deal," Zach explained.

"Thanks, but I'm fine." I know, I know, it was nice of them to be all supportive and everything, but I didn't need it. For whatever reason, I was really okay about Aunt Bertha. I just wanted to stop thinking about the whole thing. Wasn't that why I was in *Juice!* in the first place? I'd been hoping that getting away from my house, my parents, and my sniffling brother would help everything get back to normal. It just wasn't working. Maybe I just had to try harder. "So I was thinking about what you guys said about Randy and I —"

I stopped talking when Geena reached across the table and put her hand over mine. "Addie, you're not fine — you're in *de-ni-al.*" She said the word real loud and slow, as if I wouldn't know what it meant.

"I'm not in denial," I protested.

"Not admitting that you're upset means you're in denial."

Uh, except what if I really *wasn't* upset? It was like everyone else was in denial about me being in denial. Why couldn't anyone handle the fact that I was fine? Just fine.

Before I could try to explain myself again, the manager rushed up to our table, his arms piled with stacks of empty glasses. He looked totally frazzled.

"Hey, your brother said he wasn't coming in

due to a death in the family," the manager said accusingly.

"Actually, it's true," I admitted. "Our aunt died."

The manager looked like he'd just taken a big gulp of expired milk.

"Oh . . . well, how 'bout I get you kids a round on the house?" he suggested. Then he leaned in toward us. "Just do me a little favor," he said quietly, glancing around at the other tables, where all the other customers were having way more fun than I was. "Keep the death talk down. Thanks."

When the manager walked away, Zach gave me this really syrupy-sweet smile. I knew it was sincere, but still, it didn't look like him at all. "You know, Addie, once this does sink in, we'll be here for you —"

Sink in. *Sink in.* Why did everyone keep saying that? What were they waiting for? Did they think I didn't get it? Trust me, I got it, Aunt Bertha was —

I just didn't want to think about it anymore. And as the door to the café swung open, I realized there was something far more pleasant I could be thinking about. Some*one.*

"Hold that thought," I interrupted Zach in the middle of his stream of sympathy. "Randy's here."

I took off toward Randy as Zach and Geena looked after me, stunned.

"I thought she was avoiding him," I heard Zach say.

"There's nothing like death to make you start living," Geena replied. "When Buffy died — before she was resurrected — I bought the shoes I had been eyeing for so long. It really helped me through the gap."

Back home, at *casa de la muerte* — that's "house of death," but doesn't it sound less depressing in Spanish? — my dad was doing what he always does: trying to make things better.

My parents walked into the house, their arms filled with grocery bags. They were surprised to discover all the lights out and the stereo turned up to top volume playing some kind of creepy, depressing violin music.

"Sheesh," Dad joked, with a small grin, "who died?"

I wasn't there, but I can picture the look on Mom's face.

"Jeff!" she said, horrified.

"Dad!" Ben protested at the same time. They hadn't seen him in the dark, but he was there all right. He hadn't left the room all day — he'd planted himself in front of his laptop and swore that he wasn't going to move until he had composed exactly the right thing to say at the funeral. I guess it wasn't going well.

"Come on, guys," Dad said as he flipped on the lights and began to put away the groceries. "It's just a joke."

Ben blew his nose into a tissue. "How can you tell jokes at a time like this?"

Mom, who does better when it comes to the emotional stuff, walked around behind Ben and lightly put her hands on his shoulders. "Honey, how's it going?"

Ben shook his head in frustration. "I can't do it. I can't write about Aunt Bertha. It's too sad."

"Well, why does it have to be sad?" Dad asked. "Aunt Bertha always found a reason to laugh. Make it funny."

Ben shot him a look — half scornful, half thoughtful. You could tell he was thinking: *No way. But . . . what if?*

"Grief's a very personal thing," Dad continued. "Everyone deals with loss in their own way."

So how was I dealing with it?
By not dealing at all. Like I said, I was fine.
Better than fine, even. Because for some reason, I

had finally conquered my fears when it came to Randy Klein. I walked right up to him and said hello — no running away at the last minute or ducking underneath a table so he wouldn't see me. I even asked him if he wanted to sit down and have a smoothie with me! If that's not "fine," I don't know what is.

We sat there for about an hour, talking and laughing, and it was amazing. Totally natural, like Randy and I were really good friends who did this kind of thing all the time. It was almost like hanging out with Zach and Geena. Except . . . not exactly because the whole time, there was this, like, tension in the air between us. You know, kind of a *snap, crackle, pop*. Nothing you could see, but you knew it was there, especially when Randy reached across the table for a napkin and accidentally brushed against my hand. It was like turning on a light switch in the winter and getting a shock — this sharp tingle of electricity that shoots through you and is kind of scary but also kind of cool — really cool.

Anyway, the great thing is that I didn't feel nervous, awkward, or anything. And I guess some people may think it was weird that I was sitting there laughing while Ben was home crying, but . . . I don't know. I was just trying not to think about it at all. It was so much easier to think about being with Randy.

The best part was when we started doing impressions for each other. I stuck two straws in my mouth and pretended they were fangs, then started growling. Randy burst into laughter — he has an awesome laugh.

"That's the only impression I know," I admitted.

"Well, I've never met her, but I'm sure that's exactly what your dog, Nancy, is like," Randy said. We got up from the table because he had to get home for dinner. And I... well, I'd promised my parents I would come home.

"So anyway, I'll see you at the basketball game tomorrow after school," I said — I still couldn't believe how brave I suddenly was. I was so impressed with myself. Geena and Zach would never believe it.

"Sure, see you then." He waved good-bye, but just as I started to walk away, he called me back. "Hey, Addie, thanks for coming over here." He sort of wrinkled his mouth and looked away. "I kinda thought . . . you were avoiding me."

He looked so nervous. It was adorable. I gave him a big smile. "Why would you think that?"

Uh, maybe because he has eyes? Maybe because I was the most obvious avoider in the history of avoidance?

"I always break into sprints and catch rides on the back of Brandywine's scooter," I continued. It was lame, but he didn't seem to care. He just smiled back at me, like he was really relieved. "See ya."

"Bye," he said, and this time we really did leave.

It was the best afternoon I'd had in a long time. I didn't walk home — I floated. Randy Klein liked me. And I was pretty sure he *like* liked me.

I knew I wasn't supposed to be happy; I was supposed to be sad. I was probably supposed to be miserable. But I was so sick and tired of people telling me how I was supposed to feel — like it was any of their business.

And maybe that was the best part about hanging out with Randy that afternoon. He didn't know anything about Aunt Bertha, so he wasn't staring at me like Geena and Zach, as if I were this alien who'd invaded Addie Singer's body for the day. He wasn't trying to say the right thing and trying to figure out why I wasn't acting the way they thought I should.

He was just acting like everything was totally and completely normal.

And so for that one hour, it was.

Dinnertime at the Singer house. Good-bye, normal; hello, dismal, dark, and depressed. We had casserole for dinner. Judging from the stack of casseroles piled up on our kitchen counter, we'd be having casserole for dinner all week. I guess people thought sending over casseroles would make us feel better. I don't know about everyone else, but it just made me feel like having a slice of pizza.

"I have to lengthen the sleeves on Ben's jacket and pick up my pants from the cleaners," Mom said.

"Shouldn't we bring flowers?" Ben asked quietly. The whole dinner was oddly quiet, actually. Usually in my house, there's always a ton of noise and commotion — music playing, the TV blaring, Ben and I fighting, my mom chattering with one of her clients on the phone, Nancy barking. But that day, everything was silent and still. Ben had stopped sniffling all the time, but he was still being thoughtful and polite, which was weird enough. Even Nancy was staying quiet and out of sight. I didn't like it; it wasn't natural.

"Trust me, there'll be enough flowers," Dad assured him. "That's what people do when someone dies. They send flowers and casseroles."

"Yeah, this one's pretty good," Ben said, pointing to one of the casseroles on the table. Then he gestured to the one he'd just taken a mouthful of. "This one tastes like barf."

"Hey, that's the problem with gift casserole, eh?" Dad said.

"Addie, you could write a song for Aunt Bertha's funeral," Mom suddenly suggested.

Here it was — the moment I'd been waiting for and dreading. There was nothing to do but say it fast. And maybe if I acted casual, they wouldn't make a big deal out of it.

"Oh, yeah, about that. I can't go," I informed them. "I have other plans."

Ben suddenly burped loudly, and I almost giggled. It was refreshing to have something so normal happen, even if it was totally gross. Besides, maybe it would take the spotlight off me.

"Tastes like barf comin' up, too," he observed.

Unfortunately, Mom ignored him. "Addie, you'll just have to rearrange your plans with Zach and Geena," she said, and her voice didn't sound like it had for the last couple days, soft and forgiving. Now it sounded like steel.

"I don't want to rearrange my plans," I protested, feeling suddenly angry. Why should I let this — this thing mess up my entire life? Aunt Bertha might be gone, but I was still here, right? So why couldn't I act like it? "Besides, my plans aren't with Geena and Zach."

There was an awkward silence, and I could see the blood rushing to my mother's face, the way it does when

31

she gets really angry. "Well, I don't care if they're with the queen of England," she finally said. "Your father's picking you up after school and that's that."

"Look, I'm not a kid anymore," I said angrily, pushing myself away from the table. "I have a life, you know." I had a life — a better one than I'd had in a long time — and I was going to live it no matter what anyone thought. I stormed upstairs, and I could hear my mother start to come after me.

But then my dad stopped her.

"No, no," he said calmly. "Give her a chance. It'll sink in."

There were those words again. *Sink in*. They just didn't get it. I ran upstairs to my room, slammed the door, and threw myself down on the bed. It wasn't fair. Nothing about this was fair. I wanted everyone to stop acting so weird. I wanted to stop feeling like I was supposed to be upset all the time. Most of all, I wanted to turn back the clock. More than anything, I just wanted it to be a few days ago, when everything was still all right.

But you can't go back, right? That's what everyone's always saying. You have to go forward. You have to move on. Well, that's what I was trying to do. So why couldn't anyone get it?

I picked up my guitar and started playing a new song. It wasn't slow and moody, like the music that kept droning out of Ben's stereo. It was loud and angry, just like me.

> *I don't want to cry,*
> *What a waste of time.*
> *I got to live my own life.*
> *It's all good.*
> *Don't want to mope all day,*
> *Wanna go to the game.*
> *Even if it's a cliché,*
> *It's all good.*
> *It's all good!*
> *It's all good!*
> *Don't bring me down,*
> *It's all —*

I stopped. Because the more I said it, the less I believed it.

I picked up my hairbrush and turned toward the mirror to start brushing my hair. It's just something that I do when I'm upset or distracted. It calms me down.

Not this time. Because when I looked in the mirror,

I didn't see the familiar face of Addie Singer staring back at me. I saw a different face. It had chubby red cheeks. A goofy smile. And big, shiny buckteeth.

I whirled around, but there was no one behind me. There was no one in the room at all — except me. And the ghost of Aunt Bertha.

"Oh, Addie, lighten up!" Aunt Bertha cried, shaking her finger at me in the mirror. She was wearing the same pink cardigan and flowered dress that she'd been wearing at the last Singer Sunday Supper. I couldn't believe this was happening — and I was pretty sure I was going crazy. But I couldn't look away. "My funeral'f not gonna be mopey and lame!" Aunt Bertha exclaimed, grinning. "It'f gonna be fun! It'f gonna be a FUN-eral!"

She threw her hands up with glee, and I threw my hands up, too. And screamed. "Aaaaaaaaaah!"

I dropped the hairbrush and dove into bed, burrowing under the covers and smashing a pillow over my head.

But I could still hear Aunt Bertha.

She was laughing.

My mom claims that things always seem better after a good night's sleep. But in my case? Not so much.

It started in science class. There I was, minding my own business, watching Maris and Cranberry present their science project. They had done some kind of experiment to prove the best way to make plants grow. They were standing up at the front of the room in front of two wilting plants — though I guess one of them was a little less wilty than the other.

"As you can see," Maris said, pointing to the sadder of the two plants, "the geranium exposed to water and sunlight is dead."

Dead. Hearing the word snapped me out of my haze and reminded me of what I'd seen last night. Or what I *thought* I'd seen. Because, of course, it couldn't have been real. Right?

"Whereas," Cranberry continued, pointing to the other droopy plant, "the geranium exposed to lip gloss, mascara, and glitter nail polish is not dead."

Dead. That word again. Why couldn't I get away from it?

"Proving," Maris concluded, "that without cosmetics, we would all be dead."

Dead. I closed my eyes, but I couldn't shut the word out of my head. *Dead, dead, dead, dead, dead!* When would death leave me alone?

"Oh, Addie . . ."

Not anytime soon, apparently. Because when I opened my eyes to see who'd said my name, I saw her. Aunt Bertha was just sitting on my desk, gobbling a cannoli, as if it were the most normal thing in the world.

"All thif talk about death if making me hungry," she said cheerfully, mumbling around her mouthful of cream. "Cannoli?"

She waved the pastry in my face, and I did my best to ignore her. It wasn't working. With Aunt Bertha, it never did. Finally, I broke down.

"I don't want a cannoli!" I whispered loudly.

And with that, Aunt Bertha suddenly disappeared; unfortunately, Geena was still there, at the desk right next to mine. And though she hadn't seen a thing, she'd heard me mumbling about cannoli.

"Cannoli?" she whispered back, thinking I was talking to her. She shook her head. "My mom sent over *ravioli*. She said you'd get too many casseroles."

I couldn't risk getting caught talking to a ghost, so I locked myself in a stall in the girl's bathroom. I *thought* I was alone. At least, I was alone except for Aunt Bertha, who popped into the stall the second I shut the door.

"Why are you doing this to me?" I asked.

"I'm juft helping you get in touch with fome of your feelingf," Aunt Bertha explained.

I rolled my eyes in frustration. Not her, too! Even Aunt Bertha was waiting for this to "sink in"?

"I *am* in touch with my feelings," I insisted, trying not to shout. "I *feel* fine." Or at least I would if *someone's* ghost would stop following me around. But I didn't say that last part; it seemed kind of rude.

"Oh, Addie." Aunt Bertha sighed. She looked like she wanted to hug me, and I wondered: *Can ghosts hug? Would she be solid if I touched her?* She seemed pretty solid eating those cannoli. "Fooner or later, you're going to have to deal with thiff."

I know a good loophole when I hear one.

"Okay, great!" I agreed. "How about later?"

Aunt Bertha shook her head. "Addie, I'm juft trying to help."

"You know what would be a big help?" I asked sarcastically, noticing that the toilet dispenser was empty. "If you could get me some toilet paper from the next stall."

Aunt Bertha didn't answer ... but someone else did.

"Uh, there are no extra rolls," Mary Ferry said hesitantly from the other side of the stall door. I sighed and put my head in my hands. Great, just great. Now Mary had heard me talking to myself and would probably tell the whole school. "Is this enough?" she asked, handing me a wad of toilet paper under the stall. "How are you for toilet seat covers?"

I didn't answer. I just slumped against the wall of the stall and wondered if I could spend the rest of middle school hiding in the bathroom. Think they'd still let me graduate?

Okay, so I finally decided to come out of hiding. I wasn't convinced it was the right decision — and Geena and Zach weren't helping. As we walked down the hall, Geena pulled out a giant sketchbook and started showing me some rough drawings. I'm used to this kind of thing; Geena wants to be a fashion designer someday, and she's always designing her own bizarrely cool clothes. I guess I was a little distracted because it took me a minute to realize that these weren't the usual "Geena Fabiano Originals."

"I've designed a line of 'griefwear' inspired by your aunt's funeral," Geena explained, showing off her work. "Are you planning to wear a hat? Because I think you should go with a beret. It's an odd choice, I know —"

"Look, I'm not planning to wear a hat because I'm not planning to go to my aunt's funeral," I admitted, trying to sound sure of myself, trying to sound like I hadn't stayed up half the night wondering whether I was making the wrong decision.

Zach and Geena stopped short and looked at me in shock. "Addie, you should go," Zach said. "It'll give you some closure."

"Look, I'm totally, completely fine," I insisted, hopefully for the last time. Every time I said the word "fine," it sounded lamer and lamer to me — and less and less true.

The bell rang, and I looked at my watch — three

P.M. This is when my dad would be picking me up from school for the funeral — that is, if I hadn't told him not to, if I hadn't insisted that I wasn't going.

Just then, Principal Brandywine zoomed by us on her scooter. And guess who was perched on the back of it?

"Oh, Addie, will you look at the time?" Aunt Bertha said, still grinning despite her dismay. "Great-uncle Frank waf right," she cried. "I *am* late for my own funeral!" And then she let out one of those classic Aunt Bertha guffaws, her whole body shaking with laughter, like a big pile of flowered Jell-O.

I closed my eyes until I was sure the scooter had driven away.

I don't need to go to the funeral, I reminded myself. *I don't need to be around all those sad, crying people. I am fine. Just* fine.

And besides, I have a date.

It was my first real date and so far, so good. Randy and I were sitting in the bleachers watching the game and getting to know each other. Or at least, Randy was trying to get to know me. I, however, was just a little ... distracted.

But I did my best to pretend nothing was going

on. I know I could have told him everything — well, maybe not the part about being haunted by Aunt Bertha's ghost — but what was I supposed to do? Say, "Pass the nachos, please — oh, and by the way, I'm actually supposed to be at a funeral right now?" After a "fun" date like that, I was pretty sure he'd never want to talk to me again. So I played along and tried to smile.

"So, do you like basketball?" Randy asked.

"Yeah, totally." Okay, that wasn't quite true. "I mean, kind of." Neither was that. "You know what? No. I like Zach, though. And baskets . . . you know, the picnic kind. Yeah."

I was totally babbling. It was ridiculous, but I couldn't stop myself. And luckily for me, Randy was laughing. Was it possible that he actually thought I was trying to be funny? Awesome. For a second I actually began to wonder if everything was going to be all right. And then —

"Hey, chatty — how 'bout fome nachof?" I looked to my right. It was Aunt Bertha. Of course.

"If I get you some nachos, will you go away?" I hissed.

"Addie, this was your idea," Randy said, looking hurt. Uh-oh.

"Oh, did you think I said, 'Go away'?" I asked,

thinking fast. "I just said that, uh, 'These pretzels go down like hay.'" I put a hand to my throat and faked a cough. "So dry."

"Ooookay." Randy looked doubtful and stood up. "I'm gonna go get some sodas."

I sighed and slumped down in the seat. Who knew if he was even coming back?

Down on the court, the Rocky Road Bullfrogs were dominating their opponents, and Zach was leading the charge. I tried to care. Rocky Road had the ball, and Zach ducked out from behind his guard to catch a pass. He dribbled up the court and then paused, looking for an open teammate.

"Zach, I'm open!" called Aunt Bertha, who was squeezed into a purple-and-yellow Bullfrogs uniform. Dancing around at the end of the court, waving her hands in the air. "I'm open!"

I couldn't believe what I was seeing. *It's not real,* I told myself. It couldn't be!

None of the other players seemed to notice anything strange going on. Zach passed the ball to Aunt Bertha. She shot. She scored! Aunt Bertha did a little victory dance, swiveling her hips and waggling her arms, and the crowd went wild.

And what were they chanting?

It sounded like . . .

But it couldn't be . . .

But it was . . . "Go to Bertha's funeral! Go to Bertha's funeral!"

I plastered my hands over my ears, but I could still hear them. Was this what it felt like to go out of your mind?

"What'f the matter, Addie?" Aunt Bertha called up from the court. "You're fo pale — you look like you've feen a ghost!"

And that's when I totally lost it. I stood up in my seat, my face bright red and my heart pounding a million times a minute, and shouted at the top of my lungs, "Leave me alone! STOP HAUNTING ME!"

Silence. The players froze. The crowd stopped cheering. And everyone turned to stare at me.

Even Zach, who was in the middle of making a shot. The ball totally missed the basket, but Zach didn't even care. He actually smiled. "Bingo," he said, looking up at me with approval. "It sunk in."

I knew everyone was looking at me and wondering why I had suddenly turned into a total nutcase. And somewhere out there Randy Klein was probably running as fast as he could in the other direction. But you know what? Suddenly, I just didn't care.

Suddenly, all I could think about was Aunt Bertha — and for the first time, I wasn't worrying about the way I was supposed to feel or about trying to convince everyone that I felt fine. I wasn't trying to force myself to act upset or trying to convince myself that I felt fine.

I just let myself feel whatever it is I felt. And I didn't feel fine.

I felt horrible.

I felt like I'd lost something that was important, and wonderful, and one of a kind, and I was never going to get it back.

And that about brings us back to the beginning. You know, when everyone was looking at me like I was a total freak, wondering if they were allowed to make fun of me? I guess Cranberry and Maris, at least, answered that question with a big, fat yes.

"Addie, those pants make your butt look huge," Cranberry said.

"Yeah, and thanks for throwing off our team," Maris added, turning up her perfect little nose at me.

"Are you trying out for captain of the cheer-*loser* squad?"

Then Maris and Cranberry did that thing where, instead of slapping each other five, they graze each other's fingertips and shout, "Burn!" They think it makes them look cool. Usually, I think it makes them look ridiculous. But today, I barely noticed. I still had my head in my hands, and I still couldn't stop the tears from leaking out of my eyes.

"Are you okay, Addie?"

I looked up, right into the warm, deep, dark eyes of Jake Behari. Back in the old days, being this close to him would have made my heart pound and my hands shake, but not anymore. Now he was just a friend.

And, I realized, I could use a friend.

"No, not really," I admitted, "now that the whole school thinks I'm a genuine freak."

"No one thinks that," Jake said softly. "Zach told me about your aunt. I'm really sorry."

And for the first time, instead of forcing myself to smile and telling him that it was okay, instead of pretending, I just nodded.

"Thanks." And I meant it.

"I had a hard time when my uncle died," Jake

said. "I pretended it didn't bother me." He frowned for a moment, as if a little of what he'd been feeling back then had just come back to him. "But eventually it all came out. You know?"

"Did you scream like a lunatic at a basket-ball game?"

Jake laughed. "No, but I had a meltdown at a CD shop when I heard his favorite song."

Jake? The coolest of the cool? The most laid-back guy I'd ever met? Having a meltdown? It didn't seem possible.

"Really?" I asked.

"Yeah, I was so mad, I took out a whole row of Whitney Houston."

"I know!" I said, suddenly realizing that was exactly how I felt. It wasn't until Jake said it that I understood how angry I was. I mean, I was sad, too, of course — but most of me was just really, really angry. "It just makes me want to punch someone!" A few feet away, I saw Duane Ogiluy and Mary Ferry shoot me a look and then walk a little faster — guess they were afraid I was going to punch them. But it wasn't like that. It's not like I was mad at a person. I was just . . . mad. At the whole world. At life. "Because . . . I . . . just can't believe she's not gonna be around anymore." And I guess it wasn't until I said the words out loud that I really did believe it, and that's when I understood. Aunt Bertha was *gone*. Forever.

And so it finally did sink in.

"Sometimes, you just don't know what you have until it's gone," Jake said, looking at me in this really strange way. He smiled, and it seemed like he was about to say something else — and then Randy Klein came back. I'd almost forgotten about him. "So, uh, see you around," Jake said, backing away quickly.

"Jake?" I stopped him.

"Yeah?"

"Thanks." It was just a little word, and it wasn't really enough to express everything I felt, like how glad I was that he'd opened up to me and how somehow he'd known exactly the right thing to say — how much he'd helped. But all I could say was thanks. And I guess that was enough.

As Randy sat down with the sodas, I began to collect all my stuff and cram it into my backpack. "Randy, I'm sorry, but I've got to go."

"Is everything okay?"

"No, not right now," I said, honest for the second

time that day. It felt good. "But it will be. I need to go to my aunt's funeral."

"Ouch." Randy winced and then gave me kind of a half smile — the kind that says, "I want to help, but I don't know how." "Is there anything I can do?"

I smiled back at him — a real smile. "Yeah, promise to come with me to the next game."

*What can I really say today, but this is not
good-bye.
You'll live in our memory and still be by my side.
My smile is your smile.
My laugh is your laugh.
And your good heart I hope one day will be mine.*

That's the song that I wrote for Aunt Bertha's
funeral. I wrote it in the car on the way over, but it felt
like the lyrics had been in my head — or maybe in
my heart — for a long time. They were just waiting to
come out.

*What can we really do today but thank you and
celebrate.
The world's better 'cause you were here.*

You showed me the way.
My smile is your smile.
My laugh is your laugh.
And your good heart I hope one day will be mine.

"Hey, who wants ice cream?" Dad asked as we came into the house. It was weird for all of us to be home this early in the evening and especially weird that we were all dressed up and wearing all black. But I guess nothing about the week had been particularly normal.

"I do," Mom said.

"Oh, me!" I seconded. "With sprinkles." I suddenly realized that I hadn't eaten much all day — and for the first time that day, maybe that week, I was actually hungry. I guess Geena and Zach had been right; I was in denial. But you can't avoid your life forever. Once I let myself feel sad, it wasn't as scary as I thought it would be.

"Honey, your song at the funeral was just beautiful," Mom said, giving me a quick hug. "And Aunt Bertha would have loved it."

"Thanks, Mom." I hope she's right. It's nice to think that, in a way, Aunt Bertha heard my song — and that if she did, she would have liked it. She certainly would have liked the rest of the funeral. Now that it's over, I admit that I was kind of scared. I mean, I had never been to a funeral before, and I didn't know what it was going to be like. On TV they always seem pretty horrible.

But this was different. There were a lot of people there, and all of them knew Aunt Bertha, and they loved her, just like I did. And there was something about listening to everyone tell funny stories and talk about how much they missed her . . . Well, it kind of made it seem like Aunt Bertha was there, too.

"Ben, you did a wonderful job, too," Mom said, talking about Ben's speech. He had stayed up all night to finish it — but when he did, it was perfect. "In fact, by the time you finished, there wasn't a dry eye in the house."

"It's true, Ben," I agreed. "I laughed so hard, tears were streaming down my face. It really was a FUN-eral, just like Aunt Bertha said it would be."

Oops.

Everyone turned to look at me, wondering if I'd gone off the deep end. Which I guess I had, a little — but luckily for me, I figured out how to swim.

"I mean, like she told me before," I stuttered. "I didn't say anything. I mean, hello, it's not like I was being haunted."

All of them stared at me for a second longer, then

Dad smiled. "I think what Addie means is that's exactly how Aunt Bertha would have wanted her funeral to be."

And Dad was kind of right — I guess that is what I meant. I mean, I know I was just imagining Aunt Bertha, and that there's no such thing as a real ghost. Right? Well, whether she was real or not, the ghost never came back — but that doesn't mean Aunt Bertha's totally gone. I'll always have my memories of her, and so in a way, she's still here.

Oh, by the way — memories aren't the *only* thing Aunt Bertha left for us. She also left us a videotape that she'd made sometime before she died. A few days after the funeral, all of us squeezed onto the couch and popped it into the VCR. And there was Aunt Bertha, looking just as cheerful as ever. The buckteeth looked even bigger and shinier than I remembered.

Aunt Bertha had a lot of good things to say on the tape, but this was the best one:

"Now, Fue and Jeff, I'm giving Addie and Ben their own money to do with whatever they want."

"Sweet!" Ben and I said together, high-fiving. Aunt Bertha never stopped thinking about us and what would make us happy.

"Though, Addie, I'd like to give you one suggestion,"

Aunt Bertha continued. "It's none of my busineff, but that never stopped me before, right? You might want to buy some of those invisible braces — I hear they are much safer for kiffing."

Aunt Bertha winked out at us, and her laughter echoed through the living room.

"Okay, that's enough talk about kissing," Dad said. "Why don't you buy some roller skates, honey?" He switched off the TV, and Aunt Bertha's smiling face disappeared.

Everyone was quiet for a second, like we weren't sure what we were supposed to do next. But then I remembered that it didn't matter how I was *supposed* to feel; it just mattered how I *did* feel. And I felt like laughing.

So that's just what I did — and after a second, everyone else joined in.

A couple weeks later, I was back in the game — or at least, at the game. I was sitting up in the bleachers next to Randy Klein, just like before. Only this time, I was actually paying attention and enjoying myself. There was one other small difference: I was no longer a braceface. Thanks to my new invisible braces that went on the back of my teeth, I was now completely kissable.

And that's not all I got from Aunt Bertha.

"Like my new bag?" I asked Randy.

"Yeah, make it yourself?"

I looked down at the bag, which was made of itchy red wool and had an animal, with a horn growing out of its head, running on a rainbow. It looked like a rhinoceros, but I knew it was a unicorn. Did I make it myself? Well, sort of — but I had a lot of help.

"No, my Aunt Bertha did," I told him, running my finger across the wool. It had been a hideous sweater, but it made an awesome bag. It was just like Aunt Bertha always said — any problem can be solved if you just use a little imagination.

"Cannoli?"

Not again . . . I whipped my head around at the sound of that word, expecting to see the ghost of Aunt Bertha once again roaming the stands. But it was only Geena, carrying a big tray of cannoli. I was relieved — and also a little disappointed. After all, I still missed Aunt Bertha — a lot. But then I touched my bag again and reminded myself that seeing ghosts wasn't the only way to keep her around.

I smiled as Geena squeezed in between us. "Courtesy of my mom," she said, offering us each a cannoli. "Don't know why, but I've been craving them all week."

"Thanks, Geena," I said, taking a bite. Then I gave her the look. You know, *the look*. It says, "Gosh, thanks for the cannoli, but I'm on a date right now and I know you're my best friend and all, but it would be really great if you could give me some alone time with Randy Klein."

I know: It's a lot to say all in one look. But Geena totally got it. That's what best friends are for.

The basketball game got kind of boring after a while. But Randy and I barely noticed. We were too busy getting to know each other and gazing into each other's eyes. I know that sounds all goopy and romantic, like it only happens in movies — but it turns out people do it in real life, too.

And suddenly, I realized: This was it. This was the big moment. Randy Klein was going to kiss me, right there in the bleachers in front of all those people. His face came closer and closer to mine, and I closed my eyes, getting ready. *Thanks, Aunt Bertha*, I thought. Thanks to her, my braces now ran along the inside of my teeth, which meant I could kiss Randy Klein without anyone getting hurt.

Or so I thought, until the basketball flew into the stands, hit me in the head, and knocked my face into his mouth.

"My lip!" he shouted, raising his hand to his mouth to see if it was bleeding. I rubbed my forehead — I think it had teeth marks.

Once we'd made sure we weren't seriously injured, Randy and I grinned at each other. So our dating life so far had been a little . . . bumpy. That just made it interesting, right?

And besides, now that Randy knew I *like* liked him and I was pretty sure he *like* liked me, we'd have plenty of time to smooth things out. And, as Aunt Bertha would say, plenty of time for *kiffing*!

Life is a balancing act. The world can throw a lot at you — happy and sad, life and death, parties and funerals, friends and family — and it's your job to figure out how to deal with it all. Sometimes, I think I've got it all figured out. Like with Aunt Bertha — I know it took me a while, but eventually, I found a way to be sad and happy about her at the same time. And I found a way to balance out remembering someone who's gone — and remembering that I'm still here.

But, like always, just when I think I've got it all figured out, something else comes along to trip me up. Or, since we're on the subject of balance, knock me down.

It was a few weeks after the funeral, and in gym class, we'd started our gymnastics unit. This is usually one of my favorite times of year. I love the uneven bars, vaulting, and the tumbling. There's just one thing I'd rather do without: the dreaded balance beam.

Here's how it goes.

"Next up, Addie Singer," the announcer says.

I flip up onto the beam and begin my routine. Forward, back, round-off, back handspring. Split, jump, step, split, jump. I'm totally focused. I don't look down at the beam, only four inches wide beneath my feet. I just stare straight ahead, keep a smile on my face, keep my balance. Then, as the routine comes to an end, I take a run toward the end of the beam, leap off, flip through the air, and land perfectly on two feet.

Yes! Stuck the landing.

The crowd cheers, and the judges flip up my score.

A perfect ten!

Okay, snap back to reality. Sorry about that. Unfortunately, in real life, it's not so easy. Here's how it really goes.

Coach Pearson calls my name, and I clamber up onto the beam. It's pretty high, and the ground looks pretty far away. He waits for me to make a move. Eventually, I have to. I take one step — but the beam is still only four inches wide, and my foot slips off to the side. I tip to the right. I try to lean left, but my body is still going right. I swing my arms around. It's no use. I'm going down, down, down. . . .

CRASH!

BUMP!

THUD!

Ouch.

"Okay, walk it off," Coach Pearson said irritably as I lay in a bruised heap beneath the beam. "Walk it off. People, it's not that hard. Get your act together, or it's back to dodgeball." He looked at me again. I just groaned. "You did sign the waiver, right?"

Don't worry, there were no permanent injuries — except to my pride. The problem was that gym class wasn't the only place where my balance had been off lately. The bigger problem was that I hadn't even noticed.

After that first date with Randy, things had gone pretty well. Okay, *really* well. I guess you could say he was my boyfriend. And I was so happy. So happy that I wanted to tell everyone about it. All the time. Here's an example — from the morning that started it all.

Geena was getting some stuff out of her locker, and I was standing next to her, telling her all about Randy.

"And now when Randy calls, he just says —"

"It's me," Geena finished with me. She rolled her eyes, not that I really noticed.

"Which totally means we're a couple, right?" I asked. "And I think this Friday, at Outdoor Movie Night, we're going to have our —"

"First real kiss," Geena finished with me again, and then she rolled her eyes — again.

"Have I told you this?" I asked, wondering why my best friend wasn't as excited as I was about my incredibly exciting news. Now, thanks to Aunt Bertha, I didn't even have to worry about the whole braces thing anymore — so I was just counting the days to Outdoor Movie Night.

"About thirty-eight times," Geena said wearily. "Thirty-nine if you count this morning in the bathroom." Although if you ask me, she wasn't even listening to me in the bathroom — the hand dryer was too loud. "Which is remarkable," Geena continued, "considering I've only seen you a grand total of five minutes in the last week."

No way. Not possible. Geena, Zach, and I were usually joined at the hip. And I know my being with Randy had changed some things, but it couldn't have changed that much.

"That's not true," I protested. "I mean, we have like four classes together."

"Sitting in the same room while you text message Randy does not count as quality bonding time."

Zach came up behind us just in time to hear Geena say the word "Randy." He made a face. "Ooh, talking about Randy!" he drawled sarcastically. "How fun for me. Later." And with that he turned around and walked away in the other direction.

"Don't get me wrong," Geena said. "I'm really happy for you. It's just that ever since you've been hanging out with him, you've become a little . . ."

As Geena searched for the right word, I wondered if she could be right. *Have I changed since I'd started dating Randy? Was I spending less time with my friends? Maybe I should —*

Oh, speaking of Randy, he was coming down the hall toward me, and he looked so adorable in his new blue button-down shirt, I just had to go tell him so. Geena would understand.

"Hey, Randy!" I called, running off toward him.

Just then, Geena finally found the right words. "Like that. A little like that." But I didn't hear her because I was already down the hall holding hands with my new boyfriend. And as soon as I got there, it seemed like nothing else mattered. Not even Geena.

The next day — or maybe it was a couple days later; it's hard to keep track of time when you're so happy — I caught up with Zach and Geena in the hall.

"Hey, guys," I said, trying to ignore the fact that they didn't seem to notice I was there. "Look, I'm sorry about before. Randy and I had plans to walk to class together."

Geena looked right through me. "Zach, do you recognize this girl?"

Zach rubbed his chin thoughtfully. "She looks like someone I used to know," he suggested. "What was her name? Amy? No, Maddie?"

"Nattie," Geena put in. "I think it was Nattie."

Ha, ha, very funny. Exaggerate much?

"Come on, guys," I said defensively. "It's not that bad."

Geena grimaced and reminded me of what had happened just a few days before.

That weekend, Geena and Zach came over to my house on Sunday morning to watch TV. It was a tradition, and we did it the same every week: bad TV, good popcorn, and a comfy couch. There was just one difference this week: I wasn't there.

"That star jasmine can be *so* unwieldy," Mom said, pointing at one of the flowers they were showing on TV.

She was planted on the couch in between Zach and Geena, who both looked bored out of their minds.

"Stay tuned for more *Landscape War, USA*," the announcer on the TV said. I'm sure Geena and Zach couldn't wait.

"I'm sorry Addie's not here," Mom said, offering them more popcorn. "She had brunch with Randy and must have forgotten about you two."

Geena — or so she told me later — gritted her teeth. "It's understandable," she said. That was sarcasm. "We've only been doing Bad TV Sunday once a week for *two years.*"

I felt bad about ditching them, but Randy and I had brunch plans. What part of *plans* didn't they understand?

And then Geena reminded me of what happened last week — when she pulled me behind the soda machine between classes, totally frazzled.

"Okay, what I'm about to tell you, you can't tell anyone," she'd said, giving me an intense stare. "My entire middle school career hinges on getting your advice before next period —"

That's when my cell phone rang. Well, I had to answer it, right? I mean, it was Randy's signature ring. And it might have been important. Here's the part of the conversation Geena heard:

"Hello, Randy. Yes, I know who 'me' is. . . . No, you're the best. . . . No, you are. . . ."

The bell rang before I could hang up and figure out what Geena needed to tell me. Of course, I'd forgotten about it by then, anyway.

They were good examples, I had to admit. So Geena was right; I hadn't been the best of friends lately. But this was a very crucial time in my relationship with Randy. And just because I'd chosen Randy over Geena once or twice —

And then Zach reminded me of the basketball game. I had promised to come watch Zach play, and I had promised to help Geena cheer him on. She would hold up two signs that said "Z" and "A," and I would hold up the "C" and the "H." And I *meant* to, I really did. It's just that Randy showed up, and I got a little distracted. Can you blame me? He's so cute. Is it really my fault that Geena ended up holding up the "Z" and "A" signs on her own?

Back in the hallway, Zach was still glowering at me. I guess he didn't think Randy was as cute as I did.

"Every time I stepped up to the free-throw line, people chanted, "Za! Za! Za!"

Just then, this guy Freddy came down the hall and slapped Zach on the back.

"Good game, Za!" he said.

"It's Zach," Zach corrected him angrily. "Zaccchhh."

He'd made his point.

"Okay, so maybe I've been a little out of touch," I admitted, "but —"

That's when the questions started.

"Did you know who IM'ed me, asking if we could get back together?" Geena asked.

"Do you know how many points I scored in the last game?" Zach shot at me.

"Do you know what color my toenails are right now?" Geena grabbed my head before I could check. "Don't look!"

"I . . . uh . . ." Okay, I had no idea.

"Chad, and I told him no way in heck," Geena answered her own question.

"Twenty-four plus nine assists," Zach added.

"And Polynesian Sunset."

It sounded like a pretty toenail color. Maybe Geena would let me borrow it . . . someday when she'd stopped hating me. I sighed. They were right. I'd been totally AWOL, and I deserved everything they threw at me. It was just so tough to balance my old friends with my new boyfriend — I mean, what was I supposed to do?

"Do you know what happens to couples who spend too much time together?" Geena asked, in a slightly warmer voice. "They morph into one."

"Instead of being Addie and Randy, you'll become Rattie and Andy," Zach informed me.

"Do you want to be Rattie?" Geena asked.

Duh.

"No!" I exclaimed. "Okay, I'll make it up to you guys. How about this afternoon? We can hang out at *Juice!* Just the three of us."

They didn't answer, so I had to up the ante.

"Orange-tastics on me," I added.

"Great!" Geena said, her face lighting up.

"I'm in!" Zach seconded.

And problem solved. I was totally in the clear.

Fast-forward a few hours to *Juice!*

Geena was there.

Zach was there.

And as for me? Well, I was . . . somewhere else.

Zach and Geena sat at the table for an hour, staring at the empty chair. They were juiceless.

"Did you bring any money?" Geena asked.

Zach shook his head. "No, did you?"

No cash.

No juice.

No Addie.

And no way they were going to let me get away with it.

I wasn't the only one having balancing issues. My parents were both having a little trouble balancing their work life and their home life. Or, more to the point, they had both brought their work life into their home — and there just wasn't enough room.

The next morning, they sat side by side at the dining room table, their laptops propped up in front of them and paperwork spread out everywhere — layers and layers of it. Mom was chattering into her cell phone, while Dad was hogging the landline.

"Yeah, I don't know what happened," Dad was saying, holding the phone between his shoulder and his ear while he dug through a big cardboard box of socks. "But I opened the box, and they were all lefty socks. . . . No, socks aren't ambidextrous. Or ambi-foot-rous. Is there a word for that? . . . Yeah, I got the invoice.

It's . . . right here." He crossed over to the other side of Mom, almost choking her with the phone cord.

Once she'd untangled herself, she put her hand over the mouthpiece of her cell and looked up at him in irritation.

"Why don't you work out of your store?" she asked.

"Can't you work out of one of your empty houses?" he retorted, on hold with the sock guy.

"No, I can't." The person she was talking to must have asked something because then she started spouting real-estate speak. "Because everyone loves a fixer-upper. Yeah, they think they're getting a deal. Go with a sunporch."

Meanwhile Dad was back in sock land. "Fine, I tell you. Just, um, send me a box of right socks."

"Thank you," they both said at exactly the same time. "Bye."

I came into the kitchen just as they hung up. I almost fell over when I saw what used to be our dining room table. I'd never seen so much paper, all thrown in a big heap like that. There was only one thing to do: I whipped out my cell phone and started snapping photos.

"Addie, what are you doing?" Mom asked, glancing up from her laptop.

"Ammunition," I explained, "for the next time you guys tell me to clean my room."

"Oh, no, no, no," Mom protested, hastily sweeping some of her papers into a slightly neater stack. "This is merely temporary."

"Yeah," Dad agreed. "As soon as your mom —"

"No, when your dad finally —"

"Honey, I'm trying . . ."

"Why don't you —"

But fortunately their argument was cut off by Ben's melodramatic arrival in the kitchen.

"No, thanks," he said, way too loud. "Don't need a ride to school. I'll be taking my new *scooter*."

See, ever since Ben used his Aunt Bertha inheritance money to buy a motor scooter, it was all he could talk about. No, I mean that literally. Like the other night at dinner: "Could you please pass the salt?" he asked, grinning that smug little grin of his. "Or should I come get it on my *scooter*?" Or at *Juice!* the week before, when he roared through the front doors. "Sorry I'm early," he said, taking off his helmet and shaking his hair out. "I didn't realize how fast my *scooter* goes." He even brought it to my school one day and tried to race Principal Brandywine.

"Your Li'l Scamper is no match for my new scooter," he challenged, revving his engine.

"Eat my dust, Singer!" the principal yelled, taking off in a cloud of dust.

"In your dreams, P-Bran," he countered, charging off after her.

It was the first time in my life that I was ever actually rooting for Principal Brandywine.

Meanwhile, back in our kitchen, Ben was *still* talking about his scooter. Guess I should have zoned out for longer. "Yep, Aunt Bertha really came through for me. I may never have to get a driver's license."

That would be lucky for him . . . since he failed his test.

"You know, we still haven't decided what to do with our share of the inheritance," Mom mused.

"Oh, about that," Dad said, the worry lines disappearing from his forehead as his face broke into a smile. "I think a sailboat would be better than a motorboat."

"A boat?" Mom asked incredulously. "You want to use the money to get a boat?"

"Yes. Picture it. Me at the bow, you at the aft. No, the stern. Or — starboard . . . Anyway, there's a class for terminology."

Guess I don't need to tell you that Dad has no idea how to sail.

"You know, I was thinking we could use the money to get a baby grand piano," Mom said, and now her face lit up with a secretive smile of her own. You could tell she'd been thinking about this for a while.

"Huh. Wow," Dad said unenthusiastically. He faked a cough, muttering, "Boring."

"Wait, if we get a piano, are you gonna force us to take lessons?" I asked. That would be just like my parents, turning a windfall into a huge hassle.

"See?" Dad crowed. "Boring. Although I will force you to take sailing lessons."

Ben sat down at the table, searching for a clear spot to set down his food. I could barely see him behind the massive piles of paper. "Boat, piano," he said in a bored voice. "Too small. Why don't we send all the money to Cameron Diaz's charity, so she'll come here and thank us personally."

That's Ben, always thinking of others. Others — and what they can do for him.

"Charity begins at home, people," he said defensively when he saw how the rest of us were looking at him.

"Well, all I gotta say is that's better than a baby grand piano," Dad complained.

"A boat?" Mom asked, rolling her eyes. "You got sick when you read *Moby-Dick*."

Game, set, match.

"Melville was a very powerful writer," Dad said weakly. But I think he knew when he was beaten. Time to buy some more sailing books, Dad — it's the closest you're going to get to the sea.

When I finally got to school that morning, it was an enormous relief to finally be around people who weren't bickering nonstop about how to spend Aunt Bertha's money.

And that sense of relief lasted for a good five minutes.

That's how long it took me to get sick of the new topic of the day: Outdoor Movie Night. I'm not saying it wasn't a big deal — after all, it's usually one of the best nights of the year. All of us sit in the stadium under the stars, chow down on junk food, and watch a cheesy movie on a giant screen. What could be better? But that morning in homeroom, it was all anyone could talk about. Except for me — because I didn't actually have anyone to talk *to*.

"So, have you heard who's running the projector at Outdoor Movie Night?" Duane asked, leaning over Mary Ferry's desk. He pointed his thumb at his own chest.

Mary sighed, and she fluttered her eyes at him from behind her thick glasses. "Your audiovisual know-how is enough to make any girl swoon," she gushed.

Next to them, Maris and Cranberry were hashing out their own five-star plans.

"I've already planned out our picnic," Maris confided, huddling over Cranberry's desk. "I'm bringing brie, gherkins, water crackers, and pâté."

"Did you know that pâté is just smushed-up liver?" Duane butted in.

"But it's *expensive* smushed-up liver," Cranberry pointed out, rolling her eyes as if she couldn't believe Duane just didn't get it.

And me? I was leaning over, chattering to Patti Perez. You know, Patti Perez, one of the popular crowd, who normally couldn't be bothered to acknowledge the existence of people like me, much less talk to us.

And today was no different. She was filing her perfectly manicured nails, and I just kept on talking.

"So, Randy and I are going to Outdoor Movie Night together," I babbled. "Well, actually, I'll probably meet him there, but you know, we'll share a blanket —"

"Why are you telling me this?" Patti finally asked, stifling a yawn.

Because I am afraid to talk to Geena and Zach after ditching them at Juice!

Fortunately, my cell phone rang before I had to figure out a way to admit that out loud without sounding like a total loser. Even better, it was Randy's signature ring. Who needed Geena and Zach when I could talk to my boyfriend?

"Hey, Randy, what's up? I haven't seen you around today."

"I'm in the nurse's office," Randy said.

Uh-oh. I had a bad feeling about this. Before I started dating him, Randy had kind of a streak of bad luck — *really* bad luck. Broken bones, mysterious tropical diseases — last year he missed more days of school than any kid in Rocky Road Middle School history! In the old days, the nurse's office was like his second home.

And it looked like the old days were back.

"Listen, I can't go to Outdoor Movie Night," he continued. My heart sank. What about our shared blanket? And the cookies I was going to make. And our first —

"I have the chicken pox," he said. "I'm under quarantine."

So much for our first kiss.

"That's terrible," I said. "Um, if you want, I can call you when the movie starts, and you can listen to it over my cell phone. My free weekend minutes start at seven."

"That's sweet, but I'll probably be asleep anyway. I'll see you in a few days."

A few days? I wouldn't see him for *a few days*? What was I supposed to do until then?!

"Chicken pox," Patti Perez said, wrinkling her perfect nose and shooting me a disgusted look. Guess she overheard. "Looks like Randy's bad luck is back."

"Duh," Cranberry added. "We knew that the moment he asked out Addie Singer."

"Burn!" Cranberry and Maris jeered together, doing their ridiculous finger-slap thing.

Memo to self: *Must lower the volume on my cell phone.*

A couple hours later, I'd realized that Randy's chicken pox was actually a blessing in disguise. It gave me exactly the opening I needed to fix my little Geena-and-Zach problem.

It took me the rest of the day to get up my nerve to approach them.

I found them after school in *Juice!*, as usual. But they weren't sitting at our usual table — instead, they'd picked a two-person table, one with no room for me. But I wasn't going to let a little thing like that stop me.

So I dragged up a chair, forced myself in between them, and smiled brightly like nothing was wrong.

"Hey, guys!"

Geena barely glanced at me. "Um, this is a table for two," she pointed out. "I'd hate to have to call the fire marshal." Then she cocked her head, as if she'd just had an idea. "Are fire marshals cute like firemen?"

"I think fire marshals are just old firemen," Zach pointed out.

"Oh." Geena looked disappointed for a moment, then turned back to me, waving me away. "Move on, then."

I sighed. Looked like this was going to take some seriously groveling. Good thing I was up to the task. "Look, I'm sorry I didn't make it here the other day. It's just, Randy got his hair cut, and I had to make sure it wasn't too short."

Which was so adorable of him, don't you think? I mean, it's like he trusts my opinion, which has to be a good sign. Also he wants me to think he's cute, which of course I do, and that has to be a good sign, too, and —

Okay, focus, Addie.

"But, um, I came to find you guys to see if you

wanted to go to Outdoor Movie Night with me," I continued. They didn't react, so I had to smile wide enough for all three of us. "Yay! Uh . . . right?"

Geena and Zach exchanged a glance. I waited for the explosion of enthusiasm. Wasn't this when they were supposed to be all grateful and excited that I was going to spend some time with them?

"No thanks," Geena said.

"What?" That wasn't part of the plan.

"Addie, we can't keep making plans with you that we know you're going to break," Geena explained.

"You'll say you're going to meet us there," Zach added. "Promise to bring a blanket to sit on."

"Cupcakes to eat."

"Soda, maybe."

"Then we end up sitting on the cold hard ground shivering, thirsty, and starving," Geena concluded bitterly. "Sorry. We're going to Outdoor Movie Night without you. Maybe we'll see you there."

I couldn't believe it. They were actually turning me down? Me? Their best friend? Geena, Zach, and I *always* went to Outdoor Movie Night together — it was tradition. You can't mess with tradition! I mean, I know that *I* was going to mess with tradition when I was planning to go with Randy, but that was different. I had a real reason for that. They didn't have any reason. They were just being stubborn.

"You can't just go to Outdoor Movie Night without me," I protested.

Geena and Zach both finished off the last of their smoothies and stood up. "Look, Addie, maybe the truth is it's impossible to keep your best friends when you have a boyfriend," Geena said, a hint of sadness in her voice. She kept her face totally calm and emotionless. "Maybe it's just a fact we'll all have to get used to."

But I didn't *want* to get used to it. There was no reason I couldn't be friends with Zach and Geena *and* date Randy.

Was there?

Before I could come up with an answer, they turned away and walked out. Duane Ogilvy passed them on his way in. "Hey, great game the other night, Za," he said, patting Zach on the shoulder.

"It's Zach," Zach growled. "Zacccccchhhh!"

Great. Just another reason for him to be mad at me. Duane sat down across from me, totally confused. "I just thought it was some sort of new nickname or something."

I looked up from my juice into Duane's bewildered expression and wished I could squirt a strawful of juice right at his face. It would be so much easier if I could just blame him — or anyone but myself — for all of my problems.

But where would that get me?

"You're lucky I don't take my anger out on undeserving bystanders," I told him.

Duane looked at my fingers clenched around the juice straw, looked at the dark and stormy look in my eyes, and then he stood up and slowly backed away.

"Yeah, you know what, just in case, you know, why don't I go sit somewhere else?"

And I spent the rest of the afternoon at *Juice!* — all by myself. Maybe that's how things were going to be from now on, I realized: Addie Singer, table for one.

Eating breakfast in the temporary offices of Singer Real Estate and Singer Sporting Goods — aka the Singer Family kitchen — was tough enough. Dinner was another story altogether. We each found a tiny space for our plates, but that just meant stacking the piles of paper even higher. I was afraid that if I breathed wrong, one of the piles was going to topple over, and all of us would be eating mouthfuls of soggy, sauce-covered mortgage applications and athletic socks.

And what was almost worse was that the money argument was *still* going on. I wondered if Mom and Dad had been bickering about this all day long. It might explain why the stacks of work to be done hadn't shrunk any since that morning.

"I just don't think a boat is a practical use for

the money," Mom complained for about the hun-dredth time. "I mean, there's the slip rental and the maintenance —"

"Oh, and since when don't *pianos* need to be main-tained?" Dad asked pointedly.

"A piano is educational, and imagine this house full of beautiful music."

"Uh, hello?" I said indignantly. This house already had its official musician, and I filled it with beautiful music every night.

Mom patted my hand. "Not that it isn't already," she assured me . . . but I suspected her heart wasn't in it. Hmph. A boat was sounding better and better.

Dad frowned. "Look, if you want to disregard Aunt Bertha's final wish and use her money for a boring —"

"That is so unfair," Mom said angrily.

I had to do something quick, before this argument got out of control — something so surprising that it would take everyone's mind off Aunt Bertha's money for good. Or at least, for the rest of dinner.

"How do you keep friends when you, I don't know, say, have a boyfriend?" I blurted.

Dad nearly choked on his food. Bingo — that had done the trick. No way was he thinking about boats anymore.

"Um, boyfriend?" he sputtered. "As in . . . did you say, boyfriend?"

As if by magic, two stacks of papers parted at the other end of the table, and Ben's head popped up between them. "I'm glad you asked, Addie," he said, adopting his older-and-wiser voice. Ben was usually too busy to talk to me, but every once in a while, he liked to show off how much he knows about the world. He's such a know-it-all. But I paid attention — the annoying thing is that he does know a lot, and once in a while, he actually gives me good advice.

"Having a boyfriend is a delicate thing. You must make sure to always put him first. You've gotta treat him like a god, meeting his every need and whim."

Maybe now wasn't one of those good advice times because that sure didn't sound right.

"Benjamin!" Mom cried, looking horrified.

"What?"

"Addie, just because you have a boyfriend doesn't mean you have to abandon your friends," Mom assured me. She shot Ben a dirty look. "It's a balancing act."

"Sure, if you want your boyfriend to stop loving you," Ben countered.

"No reasonable boy would expect a girl to drop everything for him," Mom said hotly.

"No reasonable *girl* wouldn't drop everything for the right guy."

"Wait," Dad said, my initial question still sinking in. "Boyfriend? As in, like, you mean . . . boyfriend?"

Okay, forget changing the subject. It was one thing for my family to fight their way through dinner — it was another for them to fight over my love life. *No thanks.*

"So," I cut in loudly, "boat or piano?"

I fled to my bedroom as soon as I'd stuffed the last forkful of food in my mouth. Safely away from all the bickering, I finally had time to think.

Not that it was helping much. I had a big problem, and there was no solution in sight. So, like always, I took out my guitar and started to play, hoping that if I put my issues into music, maybe I would be able to sing myself out of trouble. I sang sadly.

Is my life all Randy?
Have I lost who I am?
If I stay with him,
Will I lose all my friends?

Hey, wait a minute! This guitar thing was like magic because suddenly, I was getting an idea . . .

While Randy's red and itchy, bathed in calamine,
I can give my pals some quality time.
Is that so bad? Is that kind of cheating?
Is that a little uncool?
Maybe they won't notice?

On the one hand, yes, maybe it was a little shady. But on the other hand, it would just be so easy, and it's not like they would ever find out. . . .

"Don't look at me that way, Nancy!" I told my dog, who was giving me the stink-eye as if she knew exactly what I was thinking and she disapproved. Nancy can be so judgmental sometimes, especially for a dog. "At least I'm gonna hang out with them, and that's what counts, right?"

Right, I decided. And I was sure that this was the right thing to do. Or, at least, I was sure that it would work. And wasn't that pretty much the same thing?

Gonna call up Geena.
Gonna call up Zach.
Gonna do what it takes to win them back.
Don't want to be Rattie; I wanna be me.
No R-a-t-t-i-e, I'm gonna do it.

nancy, bring me the phone.

I'm gonna —

"nancy, bring me the phone, come on."

nancy trotted out of the room and came back in a moment later, with my little pink cell phone open in her mouth. I picked it up and was about to dial Geena's number when I realized that there was already someone on the line.

"Pet spa," a voice said, "a doggy paradise, how can I help you?"

I gave nancy a look, then shook my head. That dog is always thinking of herself!

So I had it all figured out. While Randy was quarantined, I would repair my friendship with Zach and Geena. I would achieve the perfect balance between my friends and my boyfriend — at least while my boyfriend was stuck in his room, trying not to scratch.

There was just one small problem with my grand master plan: Geena and Zach still weren't speaking to me.

Geena didn't return my first call. Or my second one. But I kept trying, all weekend long. By Sunday night, I was beginning to wonder if she'd ever pick up the phone — but I forced myself not to give up hope.

"So anyways, Geena, I know I already left you six . . . teen messages, but call me back," I pleaded to her voice mail. "It's buy-two-get-one-free week at Lip Gloss Emporium. I'll buy two, and you can have the free one! Okay, talk to you later."

"She'll call me back," I said confidently to Nancy. I lay back on my bed and waited.

And waited.

And waited some more.

And then, at some point, I must have fallen asleep.

Because I woke up as the sun rose, my hair matted to my face and a cell-phone imprint on my cheek.

And I had zero messages. I was beginning to real-ize that this was bigger than free lip gloss. I sighed, remembering a time when nothing was bigger than free lip gloss.

Ah, the good old days.

Luckily, I had two things that would help me win back Zach and Geena: First, undying determination. And second — and maybe more important, their schedules.

For example, I knew that Zach got out of basket-ball at 4:15 P.M., which meant I was able to greet him on the court with a clean white towel, a hand-held water-spraying fan, and a huge bottle of water. Now, he didn't actually speak to me, but he took the water. It was a start.

I also knew that Geena always got a snack between fifth and sixth period. Which meant I was able to hide behind the vending machine until she arrived — and then I could pop out and surprise her, with a soda in one hand and a bag of chips in the other.

Okay, so she didn't speak to me, either. But Geena's never been able to turn down a free bag of chips.

And finally, I knew that Geena and Zach would be depressed after taking Mr. Straton's impossible algebra test, which is why I met them after class with a giant bouquet of balloons and a basket of cookies. That time, they actually smiled — and I knew I was almost there.

When they got to *Juice!* that afternoon, I was already at the counter, waiting for them with a drink in each hand.

"A Mocha Moo Cow for Zach and a Berry-ma-taz for Geena," I said, handing them their smoothies.

"Mmm." Zach took a big gulp. "Right out of the blender. Nice timing."

"Actually, I ordered fresh ones every fifteen minutes until you guys got here," I admitted.

Geena offered me a little half smile. "Thanks. For everything."

It was the first time she'd spoken to me in a week, and it was just the opening I'd been waiting for.

"Sorry I've been out of the loop," I said, "but I really want that to change. So . . . about Outdoor Movie Night . . ."

Zach and Geena exchanged a glance, and I held my breath, knowing it was now or never. Finally, they both nodded and smiled.

"We'd love to go with you," Geena said.

"Totally," Zach agreed.

I felt such a wave of relief that I threw myself at them, sweeping them both into a big hug.

"Aww, I love you guys!" I mumbled, my face buried in someone's hair.

We were still huddled up in our little love-fest when Patti Perez walked by, with Maris and Cranberry scurrying behind her.

"Ew." Pattie shuddered when she caught sight of us. "Never do that."

Maris nodded. "Agreed."

They just didn't get it — Geena, Zach, and I were the Three Musketeers again, and that meant it was time to celebrate. Nothing would ever break us apart again . . . at least, as long as Randy was still under quarantine. . . .

* * *

There's nothing better than the sweet smell of fresh-baked peanut butter double chocolate chip cookies, especially when you're the one baking them. It's such a satisfying process — churning the butter, beating in the eggs and the sugar, sneaking tastes of the raw cookie dough — it's the perfect way to spend an afternoon.

Unless, of course, your parents are "working" in the kitchen, and by "working," I mean arguing nonstop about what to do with Aunt Bertha's money. Argh.

"You know, if we got a boat, I could work there," Dad pointed out. "Get out of your hair."

Ben looked up from his homework, which he'd spread out on top of a big pile of Mom's lease forms. "Well, you should buy a share in a private jet! Then any of us could work anywhere."

Mom arched an eyebrow. "If we got a piano, Ben could channel some of his . . . *creativity* into something productive."

"Ohhh!" Ben exclaimed, totally missing Mom's point. "We should open a competing juice store across from *Juice!* Call it *Juicier!*"

"If we got a boat, we could sail off and find the lost island of Baboo," Dad suggested. Baboo is this island that Dad made up when we were children. He would tell us stories about the adventures people had on the lost island of Baboo. He thought they were really incredible and creative — Ben and I just thought they were the perfect thing to put us to sleep. That's the only reason we kept asking for them, not that we would ever tell Dad, of course. "That'd be romantic," Dad continued.

"Until you barfed over the side," Mom said dryly. Before Dad could reply, she got up and came over to look at my beautiful cookies, which were all spread out on the cookie sheet and ready for the oven.

"So, Addie, are those cookies for Randy?" she asked.

Dad put his hands over his ears. He wasn't taking this boyfriend thing particularly well. "I don't want to hear it," he said, like a little kid who'd just been told he had to put away his toys and go to bed. "I *don't* want to hear it."

"No, Geena and Zach," I explained, grabbing a pot holder and sticking the cookie sheet in the oven. "We're going to Outdoor Movie Night together."

"Aw, that's nice," Mom said. "I guess you found some balance in your life after all."

"Yeah, turns out it's easy," I boasted.

Yeah, right. Easy — as long as your boyfriend has chicken pox.

Outdoor Movie Night was everything we had hoped it would be. The weather was perfect — warm, but with just enough of a breeze to remind you that you were outdoors. The air smelled like fresh-cut grass, the sky was clear, the stars were bright, the movie was awesome, and the food, well . . . I don't want to toot my own horn.

So I'll let Zach do it.

"This cookie is fantastic," he gushed, leaning back on the blanket and savoring each bit. "Seriously."

Geena was chowing down, too, but she was too busy catching me up on her love life to compliment my cooking. "So anyway, after Chad IM'ed me, I blocked him."

"No way!" I exclaimed.

"I could live off this," Zach mused, still wallowing in his cookie fantasies. "I mean, do you think I could live on this? I mean, peanut butter's protein, right?"

"I don't buy into that 'you can be friends with your old boyfriend' thing," Geena mused.

"I would need greens," Zach said to himself. "Five a day." He shook his empty soda can at me. "This soda's dry."

That was my cue. We'd been talking a mile a minute, catching up on all the stuff I'd missed during my all-Randy all-the-time phase, and it felt like things were finally getting back to normal.

"I'll get you guys some refills."

Well, except for the fact that I was still waiting on Geena and Zach hand and foot.

I didn't mind, really. I owed it to them. After ignoring them for all that time, it was the least I could do. And I still felt kind of bad that I was hiding the whole chicken pox thing from them. It still didn't seem quite right, but now that they'd accepted my apology, I really didn't want to mess things up. Things were going so well, why bring up Randy?

"Addie."

I turned around and — speaking of Randy . . .

"What are you doing here?" I asked, totally stunned. He was just standing by the concession stand, as if he'd been waiting for me. And there wasn't a chicken pock in sight.

*   *   *

Poor Zach and Geena. They were back on the field, eating their cookies, blissfully ignorant. They had no idea that I'd fooled them. At least, they didn't until Maris and Cranberry opened their big mouths.

"I wonder if Addie could bake lettuce into this," Zach said, gazing at his cookie. Geena just rolled her eyes and took another bite.

And in that moment of silence, they heard a snatch of Maris and Cranberry's conversation waft over from the next blanket. They heard Randy Klein's name — and that made them pay closer attention. Bad news.

"You can never be too careful in crowds," Maris was saying. She and Cranberry were both holding silk scarves over their mouths, as if afraid of catching something from the masses. "Randy Klein has been out with the chicken pox, and I'm sure he breathed on *someone* here. A pockmark this late in life can mean permanent damage."

"Whoa," Cranberry breathed. "What if Randy comes back to school ugly?"

"At least then he'd be more in Addie's league." Maris giggled, and she and Cranberry started to do their "burn" thing — then paused in mid-finger-slap.

"Wait, can you burn someone when they're not around to hear the insult?" Maris asked.

"Well, why should we miss out on the fun just cause Addie's not around?" Cranberry pointed out.

"Burn!"

True, I missed it. But Geena and Zach caught the whole thing. And they were feeling pretty burned themselves.

"The only reason Addie's been hanging out with us is because her boyfriend is under quarantine," Geena complained. And even if I had been there, I wouldn't have been able to argue with her. Guilty as charged. "I'm gonna strangle her."

"Hey, let's not go crazy —" Zach began. And maybe he was about to defend me. But unfortunately, just at that moment, Coach Pearson happened by. He gave Zach a big thumbs-up.

"Hey, Za! Love the new nickname!" the coach called. "Za! Za! He's our Ma! If he can't do it . . . I'll work on it."

Zach fumed and took a few short, huffy breaths, as if he was working on making steam come out of his ears. "Okay, yeah. We can strangle her."

Back at the concession stand, I wasn't thinking about Geena and Zach or worrying about what would happen if they found me with Randy. I was too surprised to see him — and too incredibly happy that the first thing he'd done when they let him out of quarantine was to come find me.

"So, once they figured out my chicken pox was actually just a bizarre peanut allergy, I was free to go out of the house again," Randy explained.

"That's great." And then suddenly I *was* thinking of Geena and Zach — because they were headed straight for us. "Um . . ." Thinking fast, I yanked Randy behind the movie screen and hoped that would be enough to hide us. "You know what they say," I babbled nervously, when Randy looked at me like I was crazy. "Privacy is the best policy."

"That's honesty," Randy corrected me.

Details, details.

"Okay, 'cause to be honest . . ." You know what? I'd done enough lying — or at least, enough hiding the truth — for one week. Randy was right: Honesty was the best policy. "I'm already here with someone."

The grin fell off Randy's face. "Oh." He bit his lower lip and looked away.

"I mean, not that kind of someone," I said quickly, before he could get the wrong idea. "It's Geena and Zach. You know, I really like hanging out with you, but . . . I've just missed my friends." There, I'd said it. I held my breath and waited for Randy to respond. Would he be mad? According to Ben, I was supposed to do whatever my boyfriend said, and I was supposed to spend every minute with him; had I just ruined everything?

Then Randy smiled again — and I knew that, once again, Ben had been absolutely, totally wrong.

"Addie, if you wanted to hang out with your friends, you could've told me."

"I know. It's just — I didn't want you to think I didn't like you."

"I wouldn't think that," Randy protested. "I mean, you do? Like me, right?"

As if he had to ask. Like him? Our faces were about an inch apart, and all I could think about was just how much I liked him. He was so sweet and funny, not to mention cute. And was it just me, or was he about to . . .

"Yeah, I do," I said softly.

"Yeah, I do, too."

And then he leaned toward me, and I leaned toward him and —

Well, that's private. But let's just say it was amazing.

Did I say private?

I wish.

Here's a little physics problem for you. What do

you get when two people are standing behind a movie screen and the movie suddenly ends, leaving a bright light pointing at the blank white screen?

Stumped?

What if I told you that Duane Ogilvy, who was in charge of running the projector, announced the following: "Ohhh! Come here, come here. Looks like Addie Singer and Randy Klein are giving us an encore."

That's right. The whole school saw Randy and me kissing behind the screen. Or at least, they saw our silhouettes kissing. And that didn't make it any better, since our silhouettes were about ten feet tall.

"Think anybody'd want a better view?" Duane asked suddenly, and he yanked down the sheet that was serving as a screen, exposing Randy and me to the world.

It may have been the most embarrassing moment of my entire life.

And trust me, when you have a life like mine, that's saying a lot.

"Woooooooo!" the crowd shrieked, laughing and cheering.

Randy and I froze — which I guess was maybe the wrong thing to do because it just gave everyone more time to laugh. But what can I say? When you're panicking, you don't always think straight. And in my case, you don't always think at all. I just stood there, staring straight ahead, listening to the cheers and jeers and wondering what to do next.

In the distance, I could hear Duane talking about us to Mary Ferry. "See, Mary, *some* people think public displays of affection are perfectly healthy and normal." Uh, sorry, but exactly what was normal about this moment?

"Yeah, well, *some* people aren't dating you," Mary snapped, and then it sounded like she walked away from him.

"Quick comeback," Duane called after her. "I like. See? Ferry, we're good together."

And then they were gone, just like I wished I could be. If only I had some kind of magical powers, I could just twitch my nose and disappear. Actually . . .

Twitch.

TWITCH!

No, still here. Hey, it was worth a try! I began to wonder: How would I even know if I were invisible? Maybe I'd still see myself. I was about to ask Randy if *he* could see me, but —

"Addie! I can't believe you!" It was Geena, and she could see me all right, which was too bad for me.

"Hey, aren't you supposed to have the chicken

pox?" Zach asked, storming up behind Geena. They both crossed their arms and glared at us, and my heart sank. How could a night go from so good to so terrible, all in the space of five minutes?

"Peanut allergy," Randy explained.

"I see." Geena gave him a curt nod. "Very convenient for Addie and her secret plan to ditch us to hang out with you."

I opened my mouth, but no sound came out. I couldn't think of anything to say, not when she was staring at me like that, all angry and upset. And not when half of my brain was still stuck on the fact that the whole school saw me kissing Randy Klein.

So I froze again — but fortunately, this time Randy didn't.

"Actually, I wanted to hang out with Addie, but *she* ditched *me* to be with you guys," Randy said. I couldn't believe he was defending me. How cute was that? And how awesome! "Or at least she was about to, until I kissed her. . . ."

Randy was blushing — and, judging from the hot tingling in my cheeks, so was I.

Geena smiled and gave her shoulders a little shrug. "Well . . . you can't blame a girl for sticking around for that," she admitted.

"*Pfft*. I can," Zach countered. But he quieted down fast when Geena elbowed him in the ribs. Geena's good like that.

"It's true," I promised, finally able to talk again. "I *was* only hanging out with you guys because Randy was sick —"

"I knew it," Geena cut in.

"But tonight, I realized how much I missed you guys."

"Awww." Geena and Zach both beamed, and then threw their arms open. "Come here!" Zach offered. And I launched myself into the second group hug of the week. It felt so good to have things right again with my best friends. And this time, I'd been honest about it, so nothing could get in our way again.

Not even Patti Perez, who gave us another nasty look as she walked by and caught our make-up session. "Wow, Addie. Really getting around tonight," she commented, but I ignored her. It was easy, with my friends by my side.

And — oh, with Randy, too. I'd almost forgotten about him. I was about to say something, although I wasn't sure what, when Geena jumped in.

"Listen, Randy, if you want to come finish our picnic with us —"

"Nah, you guys should hang," Randy said. But he looked pretty happy to have been asked. Not as happy as I was — I couldn't believe that Geena had actually invited him along. It had to be a sign. Things were about to get much better and much easier; I could feel it. I was a little sad to see Randy go, but it would be good to finish up the picnic with just us, the Three Musketeers.

"I'll catch you later," Randy said, giving me a wave and that sweet smile he saves just for me. It was — wait, what was wrong with his smile?

"What happened to your mouth?" I gasped. It was all . . . red and blotchy and swelling up bigger and bigger by the second.

Randy looked alarmed and reached up to feel his lips. "Do you . . . do you taste peanuts?" he asked.

Uh-oh.

"I was kind of, maybe, eating peanut butter cookies," I told him, my voice shaking. "Before we, uh . . ." I couldn't believe it. I totally poisoned my boyfriend! What kind of girlfriend does that? So much for my perfect first kiss.

"Yeah, I'll see ya in a few days," Randy said, sighing. But the weird thing is, he didn't look that upset. And even with his blistery, swelling mouth, he gave me a smile, like he didn't really mind that he was allergic to me. Like maybe it had been worth it.

Well, after that, things pretty much got back to normal. Or at least, they did at school. As for my parents? You guessed it: still arguing.

"I'm sorry, Jeff, but I have to say it." Mom could barely see Dad over the mountainous paper piles that had accumulated on the kitchen table, but I guess she didn't need to make eye contact to continue the fight. "A boat is the most ridiculous, ill-thought-out idea I have ever heard."

"And where, pray tell, do you propose we fit a baby grand piano?" Dad asked bitterly.

"Hey, we should use the money to build another room," Ben suggested as he passed through the room.

Mom's eyes lit up. Dad's mouth dropped open.

Ben? Actually having a good idea? Inconceivable!

Then Ben kept going. "That we can rent out to lonely stewardesses who pass through town. I can give them a ride back to the airport on my *scooter*! Yeah!"

Poor Ben — so close to brilliance and yet still so far.

Lucky for him, Mom and Dad didn't even hear the part about the stewardesses. Their brains were too busy exploding with ideas.

"That would be perfect!" Dad exclaimed. "We could have a home office —"

"We could eat like a family again!" Mom added.

That's when I came in.

"Hey, Addie! What do you think of building an extra room?" Mom asked. She looked so excited, she was practically bouncing up and down. Now, I'd heard from my friends what it meant when your parents got all weirdly enthusiastic and started talking about extra space.

"Oh, no," I gasped, "are you pregnant?"

"Oh, no," Dad said quickly. "No way. No sir. No . . ." He gave Mom a look. "Right?"

"No," Mom said firmly.

I sighed with relief. Not that a baby wouldn't be cute and all, but come on, you've seen my family — we can barely handle taking care of one another. There's no space for anyone extra, even with a brand-new room.

And speaking of new rooms, I wonder how Mom and Dad would feel about me having my very own in-house recording studio. . . .

Life really is a balancing act.
Fall off the beam,

Then you'll get your head cracked.
You lean toward your new friends, the old ones
pull you back.
Oh, yeah, life is a balancing act.

It took me all weekend to write the new song, and I was really proud of it. I even choreographed some dance moves to go along with it. Okay, maybe they weren't dance moves so much as me pretending to walk on a balance beam . . . but still, I thought it was some of my best work.

Life really is a balancing act.
Knowing when to add, knowing when to subtract.
You're teetering, about to fall, but you're an
acrobat!
Oh, yeah, life is a balancing act.
Oh, yeah, life is a balancing act.

When I finished the song, I could hear tiny applause coming through the speaker phone. Guess Randy thought it was some of my best work, too.

"That was great," he said, and I wished I had a video phone so I could see his adorable smile.

"Thanks. So, how's your peanut reaction?"

"Better. Luckily, not enough peanut was passed in the saliva —"

"Oooookay, done talking about it," I cut in. How gross can you get?

"I gotta go soak my lips in baking soda," Randy said. "But I should be fine by tomorrow. Wanna hang out?"

And part of me did want to hang out with him. I missed him. I mean, the phone calls were great and all, but it wasn't like having him around in person. But just because I missed him, I reminded myself, didn't mean I had to drop everything. Randy was important, but he wasn't the only thing in my life. It's all about balance, right?

"Actually, tomorrow I'm going to Lip Gloss Emporium with Geena," I finally said, "and Sunday is Bad TV Sunday. But . . . want to eat lunch together on Monday?"

I was a little afraid he'd be mad or think I didn't like him anymore, but all he said was, "Totally. See ya then." All casual and happy, like he completely understood. "Bye, Geena. Bye, Zach."

Oh, yeah, did I forget to mention that I was in the middle of hanging out with Geena and Zach when Randy called? They didn't mind, and neither did Randy. This balance thing was working out great so far.

"Bye, Randy," all of us said together, and I hung up the phone.

Geena and Zach were both sprawled out on my daybed, grinning at me, and I could tell I was blushing. Suddenly I felt this huge rush of happiness. You know that feeling you get when it seems like everything in your life is falling into place, and, in that one moment, everything is right, everything is perfect? That's how I felt with Geena and Zach — with the three of us back together, it felt like nothing could ever go wrong again. I wouldn't let it.

"So, tell me all about the kiss," Geena said, leaning forward. "I mean, we saw it, but I want to hear your perspective."

Zach groaned, "Are we gonna talk about this all night?"

"Yes," Geena and I chorused. Boys. They just don't get it sometimes.

"Go ahead." Zach sighed, turning back to his magazine. "I'm listening."

And you know what? Even though he was pretending not to pay attention, even though he was a little grossed out whenever I started talking all lovey-dovey about Randy, I knew that he was listening. Because that's what best friends do. They're there for you when you need them. Just like Zach and Geena were there for me when Aunt Bertha died. And from now on, I swore to myself, I was going to be there for them, too — a best friend — forever.

Life may be a balancing act, and sometimes you may fall off the beam. But that's why you need friends — they always help you up again. No matter what.